Henry Barnard

Sketch of the Life and Educational Labors of Ebenezer Bailey

Henry Barnard

Sketch of the Life and Educational Labors of Ebenezer Bailey

ISBN/EAN: 9783337096946

Printed in Europe, USA, Canada, Australia, Japan

Cover: Foto ©Raphael Reischuk / pixelio.de

More available books at **www.hansebooks.com**

SKETCH

OF THE

Life and Educational Labors

OF

EBENEZER BAILEY.

REPUBLISHED
FROM BARNARD'S AMERICAN JOURNAL OF EDUCATION.
1861.

This memoir was prepared at the request of the Editor for publication in the American Journal of Education. A few copies are printed in this form for the gratification of the friends and former pupils of Mr. Bailey.

II. B.

HARTFORD, *October*, 1861.

INTRODUCTION.

In compiling a brief sketch of the life and labors of the late lamented EBENEZER BAILEY, the indulgence of his friends and of the public must be solicited for its many deficiencies and imperfections. So long a period has elapsed since his death, which took place, August 5th, 1839, that many of those little incidents and traits of character, which add so much to the interest of a biography, have necessarily faded from the memory of those who knew him best. The death of his widow, some two years since, has moreover deprived his friends of the testimony of one who could better than any other have supplied the gaps in his personal history. Then again, a large amount of material which had been collected and placed in the hands of the late Mr. Barnum Field, for the purpose of preparing a memoir, was unfortunately destroyed after Mr. Field's decease. And his correspondence which was very extensive, and carefully preserved, being most methodically arranged by his own hand, still referred so much to matters of a mere personal or local interest, as to furnish but very scanty data for a sketch of his life. A few family letters, a journal kept during a part of the year 1818, and some unfinished manuscripts on various scientific subjects, comprise all the material available for use.

PROVIDENCE, R. I., *September*, 1861.

MEMOIR.

EDENEZER BAILEY, one of the founders of the American Institute of Instruction, was born in West Newbury, Massachusetts, June 25th, 1795. His father, Paul Bailey, with his mother and ancestors on both sides for many generations, were all natives of that ancient and beautiful town on the shores of the Merrimac. His father possessed a small but well-cultivated farm, and by his industry and economy, like so many of our New England yeomanry, reared his family of four children to those habits of enterprise and intelligence which lead to usefulness and honor in after life. The youngest of these children, Ebenezer, most resembled his mother in disposition. To her he was deeply attached; and her death, which took place soon after he graduated, he never ceased to deplore. Two of his own children in after life bore successively, her loved and honored name, Emma Carr.

Why he was selected as the aspirant for college honors, is not known, unless it were from the love of learning, and love of books he very early manifested. Not that he was in any sense a *book-worm* in his boyish days; on the contrary, he was full of life and activity, the foremost to engage in every manly sport, and the leader in every venturesome expedition. He had a taste for mechanical contrivances and was ingenious in making little machines, and, so to speak, philosophical playthings. Even then his warm heart and generous, kindly nature made him a general favorite, and some of those who wept at his grave, dated the beginning of their friendship from these early days.

The same enthusiastic love of nature, the same remarkable order and method, the same perfect neatness and propriety, the same regard for truth and honor which characterized him in after life, were conspicuous in him as a boy. So true it is,—

"The child 's the father of the man."

He entered Yale College, New Haven, in the year 1813, at the age of eighteen. His father provided liberally for his education, and his college course was alike honorable to himself and satisfactory to his friends. Although always a close student, he was a favorite with his class, and many of his college friendships continued unbroken through life. Indeed this was the peculiarity of the friendships which he had the rare gift of inspiring—their warmth and devotion which neither time nor absence could quench, and which rendered them strong and lasting as life itself.

He graduated with honor, September 17th, 1817. His views and prospects at this time, may be learned by the following extracts from a journal which he kept for a few years.

"NEW HAVEN, Saturday, December 27th, 1817.

"I left.Newbury the first of September, accompanied by my father, for New Haven, with a determination to visit the Southern states in the capacity of an instructor after I had taken my degree. Accordingly after commencement, my father who has never refused me a competent supply of money, gave me at my request three hundred dollars. I thought this would be sufficient to pay my bills, and leave $150 to defray my expenses to the South. But as is generally the case with those who had rather see a trader use his pen than change a note, my debts were greater than I expected; so that I had something less than $70 left for my Southern expedition. But my father had gone home; and with this sum I was to make my début into the wide world of active life!

Though I had lived at home but little since I was fifteen, and of course had been accustomed to associate and deal with strangers, still I was very little acquainted with the art of living. The generosity of my father had always hitherto supplied me with a *quantum sufficit* of cash; but now I began to suspect that to earn and to spend were not quite the same thing. Neither was it altogether so easy and pleasant for one to hold his own purse strings—especially if there be nothing in it but a memorandum of debts!—as I used to fancy it when a boy. I well recollect that then, when a hint to my father, like a merchant's word, would pass for more than it was worth—I engrossed in flaming capitals in my pocket book,—

'GOD LOVETH THE CHEERFUL GIVER,'

but were I now to honor my red morocco *vacuum* with a motto, it would be from Shakspeare; "Who steals my purse, steals trash;— 'tis something, *nothing*."

But to return to my seventy dollars. A class-mate and particular friend, whose purse was not as long as his credit, needed fifty dollars to clear him out; and I freely lent him the sum, on condition he should send it back by the next mail after he reached home. It so happened that he did not return it for *eight weeks*. During this period I received several applications to go South, which I could not accept for want of funds to get there. And when, at last, my money did arrive, my expenses in the city had consumed it all into four or five dollars! What measures to take in this extremity, I knew not. I was about two hundred miles from home, without experience in managing, without money, without means of procuring any (unless by writing home, which my pride forbade) and I had almost said— without hope. I resolved and re-resolved till I found myself considerably in debt and not a cent in pocket. But conscious withal that

'A poor spirit
Is poorer than a poor purse,'

I determined not to yield to circumstances, but if possible, to make circumstances yield to me."

He then goes on to state that being unable to carry out his original plans, he concluded to purchase the good will and fixtures of a private school for boys recently established in New Haven. He found that he had been most grossly deceived in regard to the prospects and condition of the school, but by great energy, he brought it up to a good reputation, and the number of scholars rapidly increased. At the same time, he entered his name as student at law in the office of Hon. Seth P. Staples, intending to make that his profession. But he soon found this double burden too severe a strain even for his iron constitution. At that time it was his habit to study till midnight, and rise at five in the morning to resume his labors; and his health began to suffer from this unremitting toil day and night. So a favorable opportunity offering, he disposed of his school, abandoned forever the study of law, and engaged as tutor in Col. Carter's family at Sabine Hall, Richmond County, Virginia.

It is curious in this swift-moving age, to trace his slow and tedious journey by stage and boat. Leaving New Haven, December 29th, 1817, he did not reach Sabine Hall till the 12th of the following month. Here he was received with true Virginian hospitality, and soon won the attachment of his pupils, and the respect and confidence of all with whom he was brought into contact. His position was peculiarly favorable for seeing Southern customs in their best aspects, and his year's residence in Virginia was always regarded by him as a pleasing episode in his life. Col. Carter numbered among his friends and family connections some of the oldest and most aristocratic families in the state. The plantation was very extensive, the house, of the old English style, was at once peculiar and picturesque, the grounds were spacious and handsome, the equipages, attendants, in short, the whole establishment on the largest and most liberal scale. The free and open hospitality of the society there impressed Mr. Bailey very favorably; and he was no less struck with the lack of that thrift and home comfort so dear to the heart of a New Englander, which was often strangely blended with an almost princely magnificence.

While in Virginia, he accompanied Col. Carter's family in their annual summer excursion to the mountains, and spent some time at Oakly, a seat in the northern Neck of Virginia. His journal contains full and glowing descriptions of the various scenes he visited; particularly of Harper's Ferry, and the other wonders of nature in that region, and of his visit to the birthplace and the grave of Washington. The journey was mostly performed on horseback, and gave rise to many amusing and exciting adventures. In the absence of inns, the party used generally to pass the night at the residences of their various friends on the route, often prolonging their stay to several days. In his remarks upon the ladies of a family thus visited, may be traced the germ of the conviction which he afterwards so strongly cherished and so triumphantly maintained in regard to the mental powers and capacities of woman. "These ladies," says he, "show by their example, that the toilet ought not to engross the whole of a woman's life; that her mind is capable of higher and nobler attainments than to adjust a ribbon or display a gewgaw to the best advantage !"

His remarks on the frivolity of life at the Springs show an unusual gravity and dignity of character for a young man of twenty-three. After indulging in a vein of humor and sportive satire on the various classes of pleasure-seekers there congregated, he adds, "For a person who considers life too short to perform the active duties incumbent on man—who views all actions in reference to their ends, and receives pleasure from them in proportion to their utility, a watering-place has no charms; and even the votaries of pleasure soon become satiated."

Perhaps in the present excited state of the public mind, it may not be uninteresting to know how the subject of slavery was regarded in Virginia some forty years since; at least how it *appeared* to be regarded by one who had wide opportunities for observation, and who was certainly unprejudiced and dispassionate in his judgment. The following paragraph seems almost prophetic.

"Statesmen and politicians have already begun to discuss the most feasible plan for emancipating all the slaves in America. It is probable that a century will be too short a period to finish this great work; but there is no subject which so loudly and imperiously demands the attention of the American people as this. The people of the South begin to view slavery in its true light. Instead of a blessing, they regard it as a curse, entailed upon them by their ancestors, which it will require all their energies to do away. On this subject, I have heard but one voice in Virginia. *A dark cloud hangs over the future destinies of this section of our country, which few can behold without trembling, and of which its inhabitants are fully aware.*"

Mr. Bailey remained a little more than a year in Virginia, when he returned to West Newbury, and afterwards went to Newburyport, Massachusetts, where he opened a private school for young ladies. There he formed many life-long ties. His friendship with the Rev. John Pierpont, which death has hardly severed, there commenced;— and there are many others who still recall with pleasure these early days sacred to glowing hopes, and true and honest hearts. There too, he was introduced to the family of Mr. Allen Dodge, then a merchant of that town, who placed his daughters under his instruction; one of whom a few years later, became his wife. Her brother, Hon. Allen W. Dodge, now of Hamilton, Mass., has cordially furnished a most faithful portraiture of his departed friend and brother, which will be introduced hereafter.

Highly appreciated and successful in Newburyport; he yet regarded Boston as a wider and more congenial field of action; and in the year 1823, accepted with pleasure an appointment as head master of the Franklin Grammar School for boys in that city. This school had latterly fallen into a very low state of discipline, and the boys had almost held the reins in their own hands; but a few firm but judicious cases of discipline at first, soon established the authority of their new master, who then easily won their love and confidence. The power of his influence over them may be illustrated from the fact, that being unavoidably detained from school one morning, he bent his steps thither late in the forenoon, almost dreading to encounter a scene of anarchy and confusion; to his surprise, however, he found the whole school in perfect order and busily engaged in the preparation of their regular lessons, having elected two of the best scholars in their number, as teachers *pro tem. !*

Early in the year 1825, he was married to Miss Adeline Dodge of Newburyport. Although very young, only eighteen, she possessed a mind of fine natural endowments, improved by a much more liberal course of education than was common at that day. A constant sufferer from ill-health through life, she was ever the true sympa-

thizing wife, whose love and reverence for her husband knew no
bounds.

In the same year he was unanimously pronounced the successful
competitor for the Prize Ode to be delivered at the Boston Theatre
on the anniversary of Washington's birthday. A few extracts from
this poem will show that he possessed poetic talent of no mean order.
Many of the fugitive pieces from his pen that appeared in the journals of the day, were of marked beauty; and indeed, Griswold
includes him among his "Poets of America." He was several times
appointed Poet for the Anniversaries of the Phi Beta Kappa of his
Alma Mater, an honor which, however, circumstances always prevented
him from accepting.

The Ode which is entitled "The Triumphs of Liberty," opens with
an invocation to the Spirit of Freedom, and then depicts her triumphs
in the contests for liberty and independence in Greece, and on "the
Andes' fronts of snow," which then claimed so large a share of the
public sympathy and interest. He next turns to the oppressors and
tyrants of the human race, and predicts their final overthrow. Then,
by an easy transition, he invokes the spirit of Washington. The
following passage commemorates Lafayette's visit to his tomb.

> " Say, ye just spirits of the good and brave,
> Were tears of holier feeling ever shed,
> O'er the proud marble of the regal dead,
> Than gushed at Vernon's rude and lonely grave;
> When from your starry thrones, ye saw the son,
> He loved and honored ?—*weep* for Washington."

The following are the closing lines of the poem,—

> "As fade the rainbow hues of day,
> Earth's gorgeous pageants pass away,
> Her temples, arches, monuments, must fall ;
> For Time's oblivious hand is on them all.
>   The proudest kings must end their toil,
>   To slumber with the humblest dead,—
>   Earth's conquerors mingle with the soil,
>   That groaned beneath their iron tread ;
> And all the trophies of their power and guilt,
> Sink to oblivion with the blood they spilt.
> But still the everlasting voice of Fame,
> Shall swell in anthems to THE PATRIOT's name,
> Who toiled—who lived—to bless mankind—and hurled
>   Oppression from the throne,
> Where long she swayed, remorseless and alone,
>   Her scorpion sceptre o'er a shrinking world,

What though no sculptured marble guard his dust,
Nor " mouldering urn " receive the hallowed trust,
For him a prouder mausoleum towers
Which Time but strengthens with his storms and showers.
Tho land he saved, the empire of THE FREE,—
Thy broad and steadfast throne, triumphant LIBERTY !"

In the latter part of this same year, the High School for Girls was established as an experiment, and Mr. Bailey was selected as its teacher. He entered on the duties of his office, November 15th, 1825, and soon infused his own enthusiasm and spirit into the school. The number of applicants for admission, was more than the limited accommodations provided could possibly contain. But the jealousy of some of the members of the city government was early excited by the rapid strides of the school to popularity, and it was subjected to various petty annoyances, and worst of all to neglect, by those who should have cherished and fostered it.

The mayor of the city, Hon. Josiah Quincy, in particular, had never been friendly to the school, and pronounced it an "entire failure" in a report which he presented regarding the Public Schools of Boston. Though this report was published after Mr. Bailey's resignation of his position as master of the High School, and when the private school he had opened was in the full tide of success, still he felt called upon to vindicate the High School from such a charge. He accordingly wrote a " Review of the Mayor's Report," in which he set forth the facts with great power and vigor. This Review attracted much attention at the time, and as it not only contains the history of the High School for girls in Boston, but also presents some of Mr. Bailey's own views on the subject of education, it has been thought advisable to condense it, and append it to this article, where accordingly it will be found.

The " Young Ladies' High School " established December, 1827, in rooms taken in Spring Lane, may almost be said to have inaugurated a new era in female education. Here Mr. Bailey could give free scope to the development of his favorite and long-cherished ideas as to the wisdom and propriety of extending the widest and most liberal culture to the female mind. How successfully these ideas were carried out, how nobly maintained, how closely they appealed to the sympathies of the community, may be read in the history of this school. From the first it commanded a wide-spread patronage, and enjoyed a high reputation, not only in Boston and its vicinity, but in remote and distant quarters. It numbered among its members, those from the South and West, from the British Provinces, as well as from the larger cities and towns of the East. Mr. Bailey was always extremely liberal in freely bestowing all the advantages of the school on those whose means would not allow them to acquire such an education as their talents merited. Beside many others he thus aided, he was for a long time in the habit of educating without charge, one of the graduates from each of the public schools for girls in Boston, leaving it to the masters to select the most deserving. An incalculable amount of good was thus done, and so kindly and delicately that none but the recipients knew the fact.

All the arrangements of the school were on the most liberal scale. The rooms, particularly those at Phillips Place and the Masonic Temple, were spacious, and conveniently, not to say elegantly, furnished. It will be remembered that these points were not considered so important thirty years since, as at the present day ; and Mr. Bailey may almost be regarded as much a pioneer in this respect, as in his views of female education. The convenient desks, the handsome cases filled with works of reference and of literature, the cabinets of shells and minerals, the extensive and valuable apparatus, most of it imported from Europe at great cost, were new features in most school-rooms of the day, and added not a little to the interest of the scholars. Then too, if there were a spot for flowers to grow, it was soon covered with bright and blooming plants, for he was not only enthusiastic in his love for flowers, but was a successful cultivator of them. While every species of innocent amusement was not only allowed, but encouraged at the hour of recess; that once over, the most perfect order was enjoined and expected.

Justice can hardly be done at this late day, to the various excellencies of the school ; to the order and precision combined with a rare spirit and enthusiasm ; to the thoroughness in every department, united with a wide spread culture, and acquaintance with general literature. The course of instruction was liberal, embracing the ancient and modern languages, and the exact sciences, and *never* neglecting the common English branches. To carry out these objects, the best teachers of modern languages and modern accomplishments were obtained that could be procured, and in most cases their instructions were given in classes, that met after the regular exercises of the school had closed. Besides these, an experienced and accomplished preceptress, and an excellent corps of teachers trained under his own eye, were constantly employed. The aims and scope of the school may be inferred from his own words, in his annual catalogue. "I regard the discipline of the mind and the acquisition of knowledge as the two ends of education. The principal object in a well-regulated school, should not be to teach the pupils a *great many* things, though this should not be neglected. But it should be to call into exercise the various intellectual powers, and to establish such habits of thought, as shall lead the learner to regard the work of education as only *begun*, when the days of school-discipline are finished." How well this idea was carried out, let those testify who still are reaping its benefits. Another prominent object of the school, · was to fit young ladies for teachers; indeed, he often recommended teaching for a few months as a proper finale, to those who were about to finish their school course. The young ladies, educated by Mr. Bailey, were eagerly sought for as teachers in academies, &c., at the North, and as governesses at the South. His correspondence on this one point is of no inconsiderable amount, and he probably furnished hundreds of young ladies with situations as teachers. These still sought his advice, told him the difficulties of their new position, and losing him as a teacher, yet retained him as a faithful and valued friend.

Visitors from every quarter were attracted to the school, though there was never any public exhibition or display of any kind. Other teachers often came, who noted down all the minutiæ of plan and execution, and strove to catch the spirit of the place. To such, Mr. Bailey always freely gave his advice and aid, even when sought by those who were about establishing similar schools in the same city, for he was far above the petty rivalry of little minds, and was generous in his friendship. Perhaps the secret of *his* success lay in the unbounded influence which he possessed over his scholars, and in the *animus* which fired the whole school. The master's eye was felt to be on each one of the whole number, and the utmost thoroughness and precision attended each movement of the, complicated machinery. How was this accomplished? By a very simple method apparently. While the First Class in any particular branch, was under his especial charge, and each of the other classes had its appointed teacher, often when least expected, he came into one of the subordinate classes, and there would be an exchange of teachers. Woe then to the delinquent class, and the delinquent scholar! In tears and trembling, they hear their sentence to review the whole ground again, or are sent into a lower class. But if they do *well*, how precious is the smile and word of praise which they win! Never did he fail, in spite of cunningly devised plots and sly manœuvres, to appear before the class in Cæsar, as a guide over the *pons asinorum!* If they stumbled or halted, they were compelled to retrace their steps to the beginning of the journey, and so gather strength for the conflict!

The system of reviews was very comprehensive and thorough. Every book that was gone through with by a class, was reviewed to him; she who could satisfactorily recite the long lessons assigned, could take another book; otherwise must go over the same ground with the next class. The Latin Grammar in particular was studied with almost unequaled thoroughness, and, in fact was never abandoned, while the study of Latin was continued. Every lesson and exercise was carefully marked, and merits were deducted for tardiness and misconduct. At the close of the term, a balance was struck; she who had the greatest number of merits, took the "first rank," and so on through the whole school. There was an immense amount of competition for these honors; and as extra merits could be obtained for extra exercises, the contest sometimes became not only exciting, but almost injurious to health and strength. There was no *prize* held out to these competitors, some of the "little girls" to be sure, wore medals while at the head of their classes, but *these* victors, like those in the Olympic games, contended for the honor of the victory alone.

The reputation which the Young Ladies' High School enjoyed for excellence in *reading*, and in compositions, may excuse a somewhat extended account of the means employed to bring about this proficiency. Perhaps the shortest explanation may be to say, that these classes were under Mr. Bailey's personal supervision, and thus put forth every effort to meet his expectations. Arranged solely in reference to these two branches, without regard to any other, the poorest scholar in other respects, felt that *here* she might achieve a success. The reading was always in presence of the whole school, who were required to give their attention to it, and often to vote on the promotion of those they thought worthy of advancement. The reading was remarkably distinct and natural, and free from every thing like "mouthing" or affectation. Original compositions were required weekly, from each scholar, who was usually allowed to select her own subject. These compositions were most carefully corrected and criticised; and when one appeared of unusual excellence, it was "recorded," that is, copied into a book kept for that purpose, and the writer, if in a lower class, was at once promoted to the first class. Thirty large quarto volumes were thus filled with essays, tales, poems, and even dramas, many of which were of high order. Three of the best readers in the school were selected by ballot, to read these compositions, and this exercise weekly attracted a large and intelligent audience, drawn not from curiosity alone, but by the interest of the pieces, and by the excellence of the reading.

Perhaps the eyes of some may rest upon this page to whom this sketch, imperfect as it is, presents no vague abstraction. *They* can recall the kindling eye and glowing cheek of these youthful aspirants for knowledge; *they* can tell of the untiring interest which never flagged in ascending her rugged steeps. No teacher ever held more absolute control over the hearts of his scholars, or ever had more entire confidence reposed in him, which was constantly manifesting itself in various ways. From the many expressions of love and friendship which he received from time to time, the conclusion of the farewell address of his pupils on his giving up the charge of the Young Ladies' High School, is selected as showing how they regarded him.

"We are grieved that you deprive us of the advantage of your instruction. We are disappointed that you leave the sphere which has seemed so peculiarly your own. We should better love to see you continue to occupy the station for which you are so admirably qualified. We are sure that many, many voices from abroad will echo our sentiments; that many amongst your former pupils, who have witnessed your faithful exertions in the cause of intellectual advancement, observe with feelings of regret, your abdication of the seat where you have so long remained, surrounded by pleasant associations and grateful remembrances.

You go from us—how shall the mind know its home, when the genius that identified it, has departed! We *can not* forget you; but where *you* go, you will not be reminded of us by everything about you. May we ask you then to take this simple piece of plate, that the sight of it may bring before your mind's eye, those whom you now leave, whose kindest wishes for your happiness, whose deepest interest in your prosperity, will ever be with you."

While Mr. Bailey's time and thoughts were chiefly occupied by the duties of his profession, yet he was by no means, the mere pedagogue. His mind was comprehensive and far-reaching in its aims; his industry, untiring; and his public spirit led him to accept many positions which were no sinecures. In 1830, he was one of a committee to draft the constitution for the permanent organization of the American Institute of Instruction;* and he held various offices in that body, which involved a large amount of labor and correspondence. He was also appointed on committees to publish volumes of the Lectures delivered before the Institute, and to arrange the programmes of the meetings when held in Boston—which duties must have encroached considerably on his time. He was a member of the City Council of

---

* See Barnard's "*American Journal of Education*," Vol. II., p. 24.

Boston for several years; and was also a Director of the House of Re-
formation, in which institution he always manifested a deep interest,
and to promote the welfare of which, he labored faithfully and
judiciously for many years.

His literary productions during this period were important, and
involved much time and labor. He was a frequent and welcome con-
tributor to the columns of the "*Courier,*" then edited by his friend
Mr. Buckingham, and to several other papers and periodicals. He
was often called upon to deliver lectures before lyceums, and indeed
was president of the Boston Lyceum and one of the directors of the
Boston Mechanics' Institution. Several unfinished works on Geome-
try, Astronomy and other scientific subjects, and copious Note-books,
attest his industry. Besides these, he compiled in 1831, an excellent
selection of reading lessons, well known for many years, as "*The
Young Ladies' Class Book.*" This was followed by "*Bakewell's
Philosophical Conversations,*" an English treatise on Philosophy,
written in a familiar style, which he revised, and adapted for use in
American schools. But the work which most bears his peculiar
stamp as author, and by which he is best known, is "*Bailey's Algebra,*"
published first in 1833, and designed especially for the use of young
ladies—though it has also been extensively used as a text-book for
boys. It was the first work on the science that pretended to be
adapted to the wants of beginners, and its popularity was such, that
it continued to be used in spite of the numerous and more modern
treatises that were constantly issued from the press. So much so that
its publishers have recently had it thoroughly revised and enlarged, in
order to adapt it more fully to the wants of schools of the present
day.

It will be asked, "How was Mr. Bailey able to accomplish so
much?" By simple, unremitting industry, and method in all his
operations. He rose very early, sometimes at three and often at four
o'clock, and studied before breakfast. Though very hospitable, he
did not mingle much in general society. His pleasures were simple ;
to cultivate his little garden, bowl for a few hours with some of his
chosen friends, take a ride with his family in the beautiful environs
of Boston, these he enjoyed keenly, and entered into with all his
heart. His health was almost uniformly good ; he was never troubled
with dyspepsia and headache, these banes of the school-room. And
when even *his* strength and power of endurance flagged at the end
of the year's work, a run into the country in the summer vacation, or
a few weeks' gunning on the marshes of Cape Cod, would soon restore
his wonted vigor. His massive frame, and uncommon stature, to-

gether with his somewhat peculiar style of dress, would at once cause him to be singled out in a crowd. His features were decided and strongly marked, and denoted power and force of character; while his eye was expressive of a kind and tender nature. A hard worker while he worked, no one enjoyed more the hour of leisure, a pleasant talk with his friends, or a merry romp with his children.

Thus happily and usefully the busy years fled on. Blessed with health and prosperity, almost idolized by his scholars, surrounded by a circle of true and noble hearted friends, men and women of talent and refinement, happy in his family and home—his cup of earthly blessings seemed indeed to be full and running over. But a change was near at hand; misfortune overtook him suddenly, and from every quarter; so that to use his own expressive words, it needed not the assurance of Holy Writ to convince him, "that man is born unto trouble, as the sparks fly upward."

The crisis of 1837 is doubtless well remembered. Mr. Bailey suffered heavy losses in the general panic and pressure from the failure of those who owed him, to meet their engagements, and from the withdrawal of patronage from his school. At the same time, he was deprived of the income of his books, through the failure of his publishers. His current expenses had always been great; for he had always spent freely so long as he had means, and had been generous almost to a fault; and the crash found him with his resources crippled, and totally unprepared to meet the storm.

In this emergency he acted promptly and decidedly. He at once broke up his establishment in Boston, disposing of every superfluous article, including even the greater part of his large and valuable library, and determined to relinquish his connection with the Young Ladies' High School, and to open a private school for boys in the country. But his troubles had not reached their climax. The gentleman who purchased the good-will and fixtures of the school, died suddenly of brain fever, after the papers had been signed and before the first payment was made, leaving his estate utterly insolvent. Mr. Bailey was almost ruined by this event; yet he was not crushed by it, as a weaker nature might have been. His warmest sympathy as a man and a Christian was at once excited for the family thus suddenly rendered desolate; and he endeavored as much as possible to arrange matters for their benefit, and was never heard to utter a word of reproach in reference to the whole matter.

Having settled up his affairs as well as possible, Mr. Bailey opened his school for boys in the following summer at Roxbury, feeling that he was indeed a poor man and had the world to begin over again, but going to work with a brave heart and a cheerful spirit. The school was intended to be select and of a high character, and the number was limited to twenty, all of whom were engaged to enter at the time of his death. Should this sketch come to the notice of any of those who then had the privilege of being his pupils, they will readily recall the delightful relations subsisting between him and them. At once friend and teacher, they not only sought his counsel in their studies, but in all their sports and amusements. No expedition was quite complete without his presence. They loved him as a father, and their grief at his death was deep and uncontrollable.

In the spring of 1839, he removed to Lynn, and rented the estate, then known as "Lynn Mineral Spring"—but now as the elegant seat of Hon. Richard Fay—"Linmere." In this charming spot, he seemed to breathe a freer life and air. The wild and romantic scenery on the shores of that beautiful pond, might well satisfy the most ardent lover of nature, while his tasteful hand found abundant and pleasing occupation in arranging the grounds, and bringing order out of confusion. Never had he seemed so perfectly happy, never did life seem to open such noble aims. He was content to live simply and to work hard, that he might thus be enabled to discharge every obligation he had incurred; and a long, happy, and useful career seemed opening bright before him. But the end was drawing nigh.

One sultry afternoon in mid-summer—Friday, July 26th,—coming hastily into the house, he stepped on a large nail with such force, that it ran its whole length through his boot into his foot. Entering the house, he drew it out with some effort, and handing it to his wife, said, "lay that away, there may be a sad tale to tell of it." It is a little singular that he had always had a peculiar dread, almost an instinctive horror of the lock-jaw. With this feeling, no time was lost in applying the proper remedies, and in consulting the best medical advice at hand. He also consulted Dr. Hayward of Boston, formerly his family physician, and nothing that could be done, was neglected; though after a few days, the pain and inflammation had so much subsided, that it was hoped by his family that their apprehensions of danger were groundless.

On Saturday, the ninth day after the accident, the summer vacation commenced, and most of his scholars departed for home. He took leave of them pleasantly and cheerfully, giving each a kind word, and then sat at his desk the rest of the morning busily engaged in writing. It was afterwards found that he was occupied in arranging his papers, and leaving directions for the guidance of his family in case of his death. At dinner he appeared composed and calm and cheerful as usual, but it was noticed he did not eat. To the anxious inquiry as to the cause, he acknowledged, slowly and reluctantly, as if unwilling to give pain, that he *did* have "a sort of tightness about his jaws, but perhaps it was only fancy." Who can picture the horror and dismay of that moment? A physician was immediately sent for, and powerful remedies applied. The hope was still cherished that he might escape, but in the night, he was seized with severe pain and stricture across his chest, and much against his will, his wife insisted on rousing the family and again sending for Dr. Peirson of Salem. He insisted on dressing and coming down stairs, "it seemed too much like being sick to stay up stairs." Almost always in vigorous health, he hardly knew the meaning of the word *sick;* and now as he sat conversing on various interesting subjects, more thoughtful of others than of himself, it was hard for those around, to realize his danger; but *he* did fully and completely. In the same composed way he met his physician, apologizing for the trouble he had put him to, in calling him up at midnight. It was afterwards told how calmly he had inquired into the probable effect of an amputation, and how with equal calmness he received the answer, "Too late." At three o'clock Sunday morning, only twenty-four hours before his death, he walked slowly up stairs with the assistance of his cane—never, alas! to descend alive.

The next day was a bright and beautiful Sabbath. Gay flowers were blooming, and sweet birds were singing, each noted in turn by the sick man. Powerful opiates had been administered to relieve the pain, but in vain. He was able, however, to swallow liquids through the day; though when one of his little children anxiously asked him if his jaws had locked any more, he seemed to brace himself up and nerve himself to answer, "I think they are; it comes on slow but very sure." The most skillful physicians were summoned; anxious friends and relatives gathered to the house of sorrow. To each, in the intervals of the paroxysms of pain which grew more and more severe, he addressed a kindly word, sending flowers to one, and messages of affection to another. In the presence of his family he was calm, but in their absence, his anxiety for their fate, thus left alone in the world, was uncontrollable—"Oh God!" he cried, "what *will* become of my poor wife and children?"

And so the weary day wore on. As the sun set, he seemed drowsy, it was difficult to rouse him to take his medicine. It was but the precursor of the last, long sleep. The disease mercifully went to the brain rather than to the spine, as had been feared, and there the strong man lay in an unconscious stupor, breathing out his rich life in deep groans of agony. That ear which had ever been open to the voice of suffering, was now deaf to the cries and entreaties of his loved ones to give them one last word, one last sign. The life was slowly ebbing from the stout, loving heart,—

> " And when the sun in all his state,
> Illumed the eastern skies ;
> He passed through Glory's Morning gate,
> And walked in Paradise."

Of Mr. Bailey's character as a man and as a teacher, others will be allowed to speak. As a husband and a father, who can tell his worth ? To that family of five young children, the memory of their dead father, of his wishes and hopes, of his words and instruction—has been as fresh and binding, and more sacred than that of many a living parent. And in all the blessings of their after life, they have ever felt that their richest inheritance has been to call themselves *his* children. His wife too, having lost the strong arm she had hitherto leaned upon, nobly discharged the double duty now devolving on her, and bent every energy and devoted all her strength to the task of rearing these children, as he would have them reared.

His friends were deeply stirred by his death. During his long residence in Boston, his uniform courtesy and dignity of bearing, and his kind and unaffected regard for the welfare of others, had won him many friends, from every walk in life. After the first shock of grief, these true friends began to inquire into the best way of showing their love and regard for the memory of him who was gone. And they most liberally and wisely decided to subscribe a sufficient sum to free the copy-rights of the books which he had published, from the encumbrances upon them, and thus secure a sure provision for the education of his children.

Those who so long had sat under his watch-care and instruction, heard of his sudden and most unlooked for death with sorrow and dismay. But one voice went up from among them, that of anguish, mingled with sympathy. The following lines, being a portion of a poem on his death by one of his pupils, may not be inappropriate or unacceptable ;—

> " Not I alone deplore thy hapless fate,
> Thou good and gifted, generous and great !
> She, that sad mourner by thy silent bier,
> Shedding in speechless grief, the frequent tear ;
> And they, whose names dwelt latest on thy tongue,
> O'er whom a father's shield of love was flung,—
> Their depth of woe His might alone can scan
> Whose eye beams love, whose voice " speaks peace " to man.

Rest thee in peace! thou tired and trusty friend!
Shall we in hopeless grief around thee bend?
Oft have thy smiles the sorrowing heart made glad,
Thy presence cheered the doubting and the sad.
In many a heart thy monument is reared,
Whose grateful thoughts record thy name revered,
Each princely deed though done in secrecy,
Shall rise to heaven, and thy memorial be.
Thy soul shall enter its immortal rest,—
Home of the weary—guerdon of the blest!"

Many obituary notices appeared in the papers of the day, from which the following is selected from the *"Salem Gazette,"* August 13th, 1839. *What* friend wrote it, is not known to his family.

"So many tender and affecting recollections crowd upon the mind, in contemplating the sudden close of a life of such varied usefulness and excellence, that words utterly fail to express the overwhelming grief which has been brought into his own family, the deep sorrow which will be felt by so many other families of which he was the honored and beloved friend, or the strong feeling of sadness and sympathy which his death will occasion in the community of which he was so long a valued citizen.

Of Mr. Bailey's scientific and literary attainments—of his high reputation as an instructor, of the untiring industry which led him to occupy the intervals of responsible and exhausting professional duty in the preparation of many valuable works in science and literature, of the energy and fidelity with which for several years he discharged the duties of a member of the city government of Boston, of his *various* usefulness in his relations to society, we have not time or inclination now to speak. They are well known to that community of which he was so long a member.

But it is of the virtues of his heart, it is of the qualities that make the true man, which he so eminently possessed, on which we would for a moment, dwell.

Mr. Bailey had a noble soul, a soul which disdained everything mean and base, and which had an instinctive admiration for everything elevated and excellent. He had a strong love of honesty and truth. Sincerity and frankness characterized his whole intercourse with others. He carried his heart in his hand. He was not willing that anybody should take him for better or wiser than he actually was. He possessed an ardent temperament, but it was united with a spirit of feminine gentleness. He entered with zeal and animation into every scheme for the benefit of his fellow men, but he never gave way to any popular impulse, or thought any plan or project a useful one simply because it happened to be fashionable. His constitutional ardor, his benevolent feelings, his gentle temper, united with his vivacity and playful wit, rendered him the delight of the social circle. Benignity sat upon his countenance. He was liberal, almost to a fault. He never thought of himself, when he could serve another by self-forgetfulness or self-denial. He professed a firm belief in Unitarian Christianity, and his practice attested the sincerity of his profession. What he was, in short, as a husband, a father, a brother, and a friend, those best can tell, who feel that their loss in these relations, is irreparable.

This may seem excessive eulogium to those who did not know the man. But it is the heart-felt tribute of one who was the friend of his youth, and who has watched with the interest of a friend, his onward career of goodness and usefulness. Its fidelity will be attested by the voice of that community of which he was a citizen, and by the thousands of young hearts who will tearfully acknowledge that they owe to him their highest intellectual attainments and the development of the best principles and feelings that make up their character."

We are happy to be able to close this too imperfect sketch of so useful a life, by the testimony of three of his near and dear friends, each of whom was situated in circumstances peculiarly favorable, for forming a correct estimate of his character as seen from different stand-points.

The first is from his pastor and beloved friend, the Rev. John Pierpont; who knew him long and well, under every varying circumstance of life. He writes as follows, under the date of August 14th, 1859.

" When I say that Mr. Bailey was a member of my family six or seven years ; that in all that time, he had his seat at the table next to me, on my right hand ; that I thus " wintered him and summered him ;" that for a part, at least, of that time, some of my children were under his instruction ; and that I was a member of the School Committee all the time he was in the service of the city, first as master of the Franklin School, and afterwards as the first and only principal of the High School for girls, it may well be supposed that I had opportunities of acquiring some knowledge of his character.

The routine of a public teacher's professional duties, presents but few salient points for his biographer. Yet I think that there is no vocation in society that affords a more trying field of labor, or a better one for gaining a knowledge of human nature, or for the improvement of the whole character of the individual, than that of a teacher of a large common school. And, taking into view his fidelity to his trust, his full acquaintance with the matters to be taught, his *entire self-control* under exciting circumstances, his perfect impartiality in the administration of law, the facility, and the wonderful felicity with which he secured the attachment and unqualified confidence of his pupils, the invincible patience with which he treated either willfulness or dullness in the objects of his care; the wisdom with which he adjusted discipline to character, when discipline must be administered, in one word, when I consider *all* the qualities that go to the making up of the perfect teacher, I think that Ebenezer Bailey was the *nearest* perfect teacher that I have ever known. More exciting to me than to witness a trial of two generous steeds, with all the blood of all the Morgans in their veins, was it to see, as I have seen, in the High School for girls, even in moments of "recess," two of those girls of fourteen or fifteen years of age, stand up side by side, before the great blackboard, and "merely for the fun of it," with the same algebraical problem in hand, race "neck and neck" down the board, to see which should reach the answer first! No one, I think, could witness that spectacle "in play-time" without coming to the conclusion that the *genius loci*—the spirit that presided over that school, was not one that haunted *every* academic grove.

And what was the consequence? So popular did that school become, so strongly had it taken hold of the affections of the people while yet in its infancy, such a perfect *furore* had it excited at the time when the first class that entered it was to take leave of it, that, as was supposed, the jealousy of the aristocracy of the city was awakened—"*tantune animis cœlestibus ira!*"—the knowledge that, at the public expense, the daughters of plebeians could secure a higher education than those of the patricians could, at whatever cost, was fatal to the school itself. *One* High School for girls could not contain all that were eager to press into it. Even could ten Master Baileys be found, *ten* High Schools would not be sustained by those by whom the public burdens were principally borne, and because not *enough* could be done in this line, to meet the public demand, it was determined to do nothing at all! The school was discontinued. The enterprise of a High School for girls in Boston became a *failure* by reason of its triumphant success!

I never recall the image of Mr. Bailey, but with a melancholy pleasure. Like Ossian's "memory of joys that are past," the thought of him is always pleasant, but mournful to the soul. In all the years during which we sat side by side at my table, I never saw in him a *little* thing. Large, generous, manly, in all his views and ways, he always commanded my respect for him as a man, and my affection for him as a friend. During all that time, I think I may say with literal truth, never an unkind word passed between him and any one member of my family. He had a merry wit and knew how to give and take a "joke," but never gave or took offense. We all loved him. We loved him after he left our family, and began to ouild up his own. We all felt, and deeply deplored his too early death. "Too early?"—No. HE "who doeth all things well" never sends his angel, Death, to call any one of his children home *too early.* 'The righteous perisheth, and no man layeth it to heart; and merciful men are taken away, none considering that the righteous are taken away from the evil to come.'"

The following is from a lady, for several years associated with Mr. Bailey in the Young Ladies' High School, of rare talents, and known on both sides of the Atlantic for her philanthropic labors, and her literary efforts. Educated in England, and spending a great portion of her subsequent life on the continent, her views possess a double value, as being the conclusions of a large and liberal mind, and as also showing the strong and lasting influence exerted by Mr. Bailey over those with whom he was once brought in contact. Writing under the date of September 1st, 1859, she says:—

"My mind is profoundly stirred by the information that a memoir of Mr. Bailey is about being prepared. No one will read it with a deeper interest than myself, for no one more truly appreciated his educational influence, or has been more greatly benefited by it. That wonderfully influential faculty was in him a thing apart and unlike any power of the kind I ever saw in another. It combined all the qualifications that go to make up the high military genius. It was at once exact and enthusiastic; scientific and imaginative. Without ever having pronounced the words, ' Woman's Rights.'—*he* laid the foundations of the broadest and truest woman's rights, for New England. The contest he maintained with the mayor of Boston, in behalf of the daughters of Boston, and the manner in which he asserted their right to a high public instruction, did a work which will never die out in New England, but which will be communicated with unceasing power from age to age.

I remember many of his judgments given in the spirit of an observer of the nicest qualifications both philosophical and physiological, and in the happiest popular manner. It was always his way to *settle* a question, rather than *debate* it. Of the comparative powers of girls and boys as students, of which he was so amply qualified to judge by his great experience in teaching both, he said, 'girls beat boys of the same age, at the same literary and mathematical studies, but they *cry* over them more." This remark covers the whole ground of difference of organization.

I should never be weary of telling of his unequaled method, by which, as a general reviewing and employing an army, he could deal with hundreds like one—of his inspiring sympathy, of his skill in imparting instruction, of his bounty in gratuitously bestowing it on the deserving. *He* knew of no infantine or feminine road to learning, any more than a royal one; and that unconsciousness has been a blessing to thousands of the New England youth of both sexes, whom he knew how to stimulate and inspire with his own profound sense of realities, and hatred of pretence, cant, and sentimentalism.

May the time soon come, when such men may look to the presidency of Harvard, Yale, and other kindred institutions, as the natural reward of their educational labors and the natural field for ever-renewed exertions. Happy indeed, would be that literary institution, that could secure the services of such a man as EBENEZER BAILEY!"

We will conclude with the letter before alluded to, of his brother-in-law, the Hon. Allen W. Dodge. This letter is dated March 27th, 1861, and will be especially appreciated by those who know Mr. Dodge's cool, clear judgment and keenness of discernment. The analysis which he gives of Mr. Bailey's character and mental habits, is peculiarly valuable, and will be acknowledged by his friends to be a tribute to his memory no less just, than grateful.

"My first acquaintance with the late Ebenezer Bailey, commenced somewhere about the year 1820, when he was teaching in Newburyport. His success here was very flattering, and he soon received an appointment as head-master of the Franklin Grammar School, Boston. He at once entered on his duties in this new position, and taught there with great and increasing success for several years. Afterwards he was appointed principal of the High School for girls in that city, an institution that owed its establishment mainly to his advocacy of it in the journals of the day.

Under his management, the experiment—for it was the first attempt of the kind in New England—became a success, and the daughters of the humblest citizen here received at the public expense, an education as thorough and as valuable, as could otherwise be obtained only at great cost, and by a favored few. But this did not avail to save the school from an untimely end; indeed it was perhaps the chief cause of its destruction. Mr. Bailey always maintained that this was accomplished by the influence of Josiah Quincy

Sen., who was then mayor of Boston, and publicly proclaimed this conviction in a pamphlet of marked ability, in which he sharply reviewed mayor Quincy's proceedings.

On resigning his position as head master of the High School for girls, he immediately opened a private school for young ladies in Boston.   To rehearse the history of the 'Young Ladies' High School,' would be to tell the early history of many of the finest minds that have graced our New England homes or adorned her literature, for the last quarter of a century.   But in schools as in every thing else, 'the fashion thereof passeth away,' and this circumstance, together with the general stagnation of business during the great panic of 1837, led him to quit the scene of his greenest laurels, and of so many pleasant associations, and to open a home boarding school for boys in a retired and romantic spot, then known as the 'Mineral Spring,' in Lynn, Massachusetts.

The chief cause of this great change of life in Mr. Bailey, was the pecuniary embarrassments that had now overtaken him.   His school had been carried on in a style regardless of expense; the best teachers, the best equipments, the best of every thing needed for its success, were always procured, if possible.   His own style of living too, had been on the most liberal scale; for one of his means, he lived like a prince, not, however, for his own selfish enjoyment.   Large and extravagant entertainments were positively distasteful to him, but his every-day hospitality was unbounded.   His house, his table, his books, and his purse were always open to his friends, and no man had warmer or truer friends.   So, finding himself unable to keep up the expense of a city home according to his ideal, he withdrew to the simpler life of the country.

Hardly, however, had his new career opened before him, when he was suddenly stricken down with that dreadful disease, the lock-jaw. I was with him during the last sad days of his life.   He knew the peril he was in and took all known precautions, under the best of medical advice and skill, to escape it.   But all in vain—the strong man bowed before the fell destroyer.   During the intervals of paroxysms of pain, he was calm, resigned, and even cheerful.   On observing to him the mysterious nature of his disease, a mere incision of the nerves by a nail—and the whole system deranged, 'I was just thinking' he replied, 'of those beautiful lines of Dr. Watts,'

> 'Strange that a harp of a thousand strings,
> Should keep in tune so long !'

He then spoke of his approaching death with the same calmness—

spoke of it, and of his happy family so soon to be bereaved. Never was a tenderer husband and father, and to leave his wife with shattered health, those five little children needing more than a mother's care—*this* was the bitterest drop in his cup of agony—which absorbed all the rest. On assuring him that I would endeavor to be to them a father and a protector, he grasped me firmly by the hand saying, 'Then I can die in peace.' And so this friend of his race, this man of letters and of wisdom, this illustrious teacher of the youth of his time, passed away from earth; but the good that he did, lives after him, and will yet live through many generations.

To me his memory is as fresh as if were but yesterday he was here. His noble form, his commanding stature, his broad, manly chest; his strongly marked features, seem yet present before me. I hear his sonorous voice, his well-articulated words, his cheerful and contagious laugh, so hearty and spirit-stirring. I listen to the anecdote he relates with such spirit and interest to illustrate some point in our conversation. I hear his clear and simple explanation of some scientific fact or law of nature. For the study of these, he had a great passion. Astronomy, chemistry, botany and the natural sciences generally, were known to him, not as a dry series of names and formulas, but as practical truths to be applied to every day life.

As a scholar his learning was varied, extensive and thorough. Always a *student*, he scorned to pretend to knowledge which he did not possess. Least of all did he make a parade of his learning. In pure mathematics he was eminently an adept. As a poet, he held no mean rank, even in New England. His ear was quick to detect an error of rhythm, or a word mispronounced. His sense of grammatical construction was as unerring as an instinct. Indeed, if he had one favorite study more than another, it was philology. His library possessed a rare and valuable collection of standard authorities on the use of language; and his critical eye and taste filled the margins of the books he read with notes and queries. His literary taste was nice and discriminating, cultivated by long and patient discipline, and remarkably free from all capriciousness. His style of writing was clear and simple, yet always fresh and vigorous; and had he devoted himself to literature, he would have been as widely known as an author, as he now is as a teacher. In this respect, I can not speak of his character from personal knowledge. The illustrations of his success are to be found in the hundreds of young persons educated by him, and living witnesses of his power over the mind and the heart. I am persuaded that not one of these would fail to bear testimony to his faithful, devoted, and enthusiastic endeavors to promote their growth in knowledge and in virtue.

But it is as a man and a friend, as a companion in social intercourse, that I would essay to present him to the teachers of the present day. I knew him intimately for twenty years; most of that time I was with him more or less, and for the remainder was in frequent correspondence with him. I never knew a man so uniformly cheerful, often under the most trying circumstances, so kind and attentive to the feelings and the happiness of others. Full of interesting knowledge, with a never-failing vein of wit and vivacity, he at once charmed and instructed. And he was ever ready himself to listen to others, and be instructed by them in turn. He never carried the *schoolmaster* into the private walks of life, but entered warmly and appreciatingly into the topics of the day, and imparted fresh interest to their discussion. So genial his disposition—so open-hearted and free from deceit—he was the very soul of honor and honesty in his dealings with others. He commanded their respect, and enjoyed their confidence, while he received their most devoted and heart-felt affection. In all my intercourse with him, I never knew him to give way to unbecoming anger, or to utter a judgment of others, that he would wish unsaid. He was deliberate in his words and acts to a remarkable degree. His temper, though warm, was under the most perfect control, even in the most trying circumstances. He was tolerant of the religious and political views of others, however much they might differ from his own. While a firm believer himself in the liberal views of Christianity, he held in high esteem the members of all other denominations, and in return received their confidence and support. No man had a deeper respect for the Bible than he, or had more thoroughly read and studied its sacred pages.

But I must close this brief sketch, hardly drawn perhaps with sufficient distinctness to mark the individuality of one with whom I took sweet counsel in the earlier part of my life, and the fragrance of whose memory has followed me along its subsequent pathway, and will continue with me to its end."

APPENDIX.

Extracts from "Review of the Mayor's Report."

PRINTED, 1828.

HIGH SCHOOL FOR GIRLS.

The Report of Mr. Quincy recommending various IMPROVEMENTS in our system consists of three parts,—as it relates to the High School for Girls, the Grammar and Writing Schools, and the Primary Schools,—each of which would afford matter for copious remarks, perhaps for severe animadversion. It is no part of my plan, however, to examine his project, so far as it relates to what he calls, by way of emphasis, "the Common Schools." But having been appointed by the School Committee to conduct the experiment of the High School for Girls,—having devoted my time and strength and all my energies to this service for nearly two years,—and having been intimately acquainted with the whole history and progress of the institution, I feel myself called upon to expose the fallacy of Mr. Quincy's arguments, by which he would satisfy the public that "the result of the experiment has been an entire FAILURE:"—that such an institution is from its very nature "impracticable" in this city! This renders it a solemn duty to disabuse the public by showing them the other side of the picture, and, moreover, many of those friends whose opinions I am most accustomed to respect, have urged this duty upon me. For myself, I need not say, that I *can* be influenced by *no* interested motive,—my present position being far more eligible than any which the School Committee have it in their power to bestow. If, therefore, I have any personal interest in the matter, it is that the High School for Girls should be discontinued.

The subject requires that I "use great plainness of speech;" but I would not willingly forget the respect due to one who "has done the State some service,"—more especially as I have no personal animosity towards Mr. Quincy. In this discussion, he is regarded only as a public man, intrusted with important interests by his fellow citizens, and exerting an active and powerful influence upon the institutions of the city. The extent to which instruction should be carried at the public expense, is a question fairly open for discussion on general principles; and one on which intelligent and patriotic men may very honestly entertain different opinions· Whether, in particular, it was expedient to institute the High School for Girls,—and whether, after it was instituted, it ought to have been sustained,—are questions worthy of a free investigation, but they ought to be met in a manly, open and ingenuous manner. It may not be expedient to support a High School for Girls,—but it *is* expedient that the citizens be correctly informed on the subject,—and it is *not* right that the institution should be put down by "indirection." I do not complain of Mr. Quincy that he has been adverse to that school, from the very day when it was first proposed,—he had an unquestionable right to be opposed to the "experiment;"—but I do complain of him because he has not been an open and generous enemy to it,—because he has not pursued a course worthy of the institution, of himself, of the city over which he presides.

The people of Boston have been accustomed almost to venerate their public schools, for they have regarded them as a rich inheritance bequeathed to them by their ancestors. They have *loved* these institutions, for the influence they have exerted on the minds and manners and hearts of their children; and although they have never supposed their schools to be perfect, still they have been *proud* of them. They have paid liberally and with a willing hand for their support, and have felt them to be noble monuments of an enlightened policy. Nor has this feeling been confined to citizens of Boston alone. Their system of free schools has excited the admiration of intelligent strangers, not only from different parts of our own country but from Europe, and has been regarded as a model, well worthy of being attentively studied. It is not generally known except to their teachers, how often the public schools of this city are visited by persons from abroad, interested in the subject of education. While the High School for Girls was in operation, it was thus visited almost daily. It happened not unfrequently, that many gentlemen were present at the same time, who had come from different and from distant parts of the country for the single purpose of examining the methods of education pursued in this city. Among these were often to be seen the accredited agents of public institutions from different cities.

Knowing these things, it was with a feeling of mortification,—of astonishment,—that I read the Report of Mr. Quincy. I was not prepared to hear, from the Chairman of the School Committee, that our whole system of public education is radically wrong,—that we are vastly behind the age in this respect,—and that our schools are so essentially defective, that their present arrangements must be torn up, root and branch, to make way for a new organization. No one will deny that these schools have some defects which demand a remedy. But these are merely accidental faults, which can be removed without destroying the integrity of the whole system,—a system which has been advancing towards perfection, under the fostering care and wisdom of successive generations; and which, if it has not produced many FRANKLINS, has at least rendered the population of Boston proverbial for their love of order, and their general intelligence.

It is true the free schools of Boston are very liberally supported, and the people wish them to be so. *They* do not complain of the expense, for they want a *good* education for their children, not a cheap one. No doubt, they wish their rulers, by a prudent and economical course of policy, to husband well the resources of the city, and not squander them on extravagant schemes and doubtful speculations. I speak now of the great body of the people, upon whom the public burdens fall with the greatest weight; for I am not ignorant there are some individuals who think too much money is expended for the schools. I have heard such an opinion avowed by more than one member of the City Government,—*and by no one else.* In that quarter it has been said, that the public schools should be merely eleemosynary establishments, where nothing but the lowest elements of learning should be doled out to the children of poverty! The municipal officer who avows such a sentiment in this community, must be respected, at least, for his fairness and candor. From such a man, the friends of a liberal system of education have nothing to fear, for they always know where to find him. But it is from those who hold the same opinion, but have not the courage to avow it,—from those who would reduce the schools from their present rank by "indirection,"—that real danger is to be apprehended. And that this is the design of the present project of the Mayor, however it may be disguised and glossed over, is but too evident. He talks much indeed about "raising the standard of our common schools;" but how does he propose to do it? Why, simply by adding a splendid list of new studies, dismissing half the present teachers, and making them like the Monitorial Schools of New York! Nothing could be easier. Did our worthy Mayor ever see those same Monitorial schools which he is holding up to our view as models? or did he suppose no person in Boston had ever seen them?

The history of Mr. Quincy's Report is understood to be as follows: After I had tendered to the School Committee my resignation as Master of the High School for Girls, a sub-committee was raised to take into consideration the expediency of continuing the school. This committee made a report early in the month of December, which recommended that the school should be sustained. Upon the question of accepting this report, the committee were equally divided; and Mr. Quincy *shrunk from the performance of his official duty, as Chairman of the School Committee, and declined giving his casting vote!* This fact is worthy of being remembered. The fate of the school was then thrown wholly into his hands,—it hung on his individual decision. By raising his finger he could have saved it, and he would not. Now that he was called upon to act openly and decidedly, he shrunk back. His cherished feelings of hostility to the school would not permit him to sustain it; and *at that particular juncture*, he might have found it inconvenient to incur the responsibility of putting it down; for it was a popular institution, and *during the month of December*, there was not a little excitement on the subject. It was finally moved to refer the report to the next School Committee. On this question, the members were again equally divided, and the Mayor *gave his casting vote for postponement.* Soon after the organization of the present Board, the subject was again referred to a sub-committee, of which Mr. Quincy was the Chairman; and the result of their labors,—or rather of *his* labors,—will be found in the report now under consideration; the real object of which is to discontinue the High School for Girls, and the incidental to "improve and elevate" the other schools. It has somehow happened, however, that the *accidental* circumstance has given a name to the document, and that the Committee appointed to examine into the expediency of continuing the High School for Girls, have reported on another and quite a different subject! The explanation is, that while Mr. Quincy had neither forgotten this school, nor his settled determination to put it down, he could not venture upon this measure —*even after he had secured his election for another year*—without informing the public that he was about to substitute something better in its place; and hence brings into review our whole system of Public Schools.

Grant that the High School for Girls was but an "experiment," it will not be denied that it was a very important one. It was the *first* institution of the kind; and as such, not only excited a lively interest in our own community and country, but even in England, and on the Continent, the establishment of this school was honorably noticed in the public journals. It is highly important, therefore, to the general interests of female education, that the true result of this "experiment" should be known. If it were indeed a "failure,"—that is, if our own experience has made it certain that it is either inexpedient or impracticable to extend to females a liberal course of education,—it should warn others not to make the attempt. But if the "failure" proceeded from other causes, it should be exposed, that the great cause of female education may suffer no detriment.

Can an "experiment" be said to have "failed" in any correct sense of the term, when it has fully answered all the purposes for which it was instituted? That this has been the fact with respect to the High School for Girls may be shown from the following abstract of the views and motives of the School Committee in undertaking the "experiment:"

1. On principles of general expediency, it was intended to make more liberal provisions for female education in the city, by furnishing the girls a school, "similar to the High School for Boys, as an object of ambition and profitable employment for three years of life, now inadequately occupied."

As to the success of the school so far as the proficiency of the scholars should be taken into the account, it is not for me to express an opinion. This point is willingly left to the decision of the public. Even Mr. Quincy has graciously allowed that the "conduct of the school was very satisfactory both to the parents of the children and to the School Committee." And that "as an object of ambition," its influence was even greater than had been anticipated, is evident enough from the whole tenor of the Mayor's report. In these respects, therefore, the expectations of the School Committee were fully realized; there was no failure here.

2. The Committee thought "it would have a happy effect in qualifying females, to become instructors in our public schools."

That it has had "this happy effect," is manifest from the fact that several of the young ladies, educated in the High School, are now engaged in teaching; while many others, thoroughly qualified for the business, would gladly be thus employed. Here, then, there was no "failure."

3. The Committee supposed "it would put to test the usefulness of monitorial or mutual instruction, and the practicability of introducing it into our public schools." Mr. Quincy himself says "it effectually proved the advantage of the system of monitorial or mutual instruction;" and that it proved its "practicability" may be safely inferred from the strenuous efforts he is now making to accomplish that purpose. Surely, there was no "failure" here.

To what, then, is the "failure of the experiment" to be attributed? In what did it consist? The report states several circumstances,—all connected with the necessary accommodations for the school,—in which the projects of the committee seem to have failed.

In instituting a High School for Girls, of course it was supposed that a house for its accommodation would be eventually wanted; though not absolutely necessary "the first year of its operation." For *one* year,—*one* class,—an unoccupied story in the Bowdoin school-house would be sufficient. Who, for a moment, dreamed that the incapacity of that one room to accommodate the *three* annual classes would be construed into a failure of the project? Yet such has been the case. And more, when the sub-committee of the High School for Girls made their report in August, 1826, and stated that "so far the experiment had succeeded, beyond the most sanguine expectations of those who had first proposed it;" that "the interest of the pupils had been so much excited, the attendance so constant, and the desire of remaining in the school so great, as often to lead to a great personal sacrifice of ease and pleasure, rather than forego its benefits;" that "the school had so firmly established itself in the confidence and affections of the citizens, as to encourage them to ask for an appropriation for its continued support and permanent accommodation;"—Mr. Quincy, the Chairman of the Committee to whom this report was referred, delayed making a report till *the October following*. And although the exigencies of the school were pressing, he postponed, in that report, making any provisions for the school, until the result of the next examination of candidates for admission, should be known! leaving the question of a room to accommodate the scholars to be settled *after* they were ready to occupy it!

In the same month, Mr. Quincy addressed a circular to the Masters of the Grammar Schools, from which the following extracts are made:

"Suggestions having been made that the effect of the High School for Girls is disadvantageous upon the character and prospects of the other schools in this metropolis:

1. By diminishing the zeal of the generality of the other females in these schools.
2. By taking away their most exemplary scholars.
3. By disqualifying the masters from a gradual introduction into these schools of the monitorial system, by thus removing from them the class of females best qualified to become monitors.
4. By reducing the other schools from the highest to a secondary grade, by early depriving them of those scholars in whom they have the greatest pride, and who are of the highest promise.

I am therefore directed to inquire whether there is any foundation for these suggestions, and what effect has been produced by the High School for Girls on the character and prospects of your school." JOSIAH QUINCY, *Chairman School Committee.*

No one can mistake the object of this most remarkable circular. First, "suggestions" are made to the masters, that the effect of the High School has been "disadvantageous" to the schools under their immediate care! By whom had these suggestions been made? Who was the author of them? Why was not the same alarm sounded with respect to the Latin and English High Schools which must have produced the same effect? I must acknowledge myself ignorant on what principle of human nature "the zeal of the best scholars would be *diminished*" by the prospect of an admission to the High School as a reward for their exertions! Finally the masters are reminded—all in sheer good-nature and simplicity of purpose, no doubt—that their schools were reduced to a "secondary grade," and that their most "exemplary scholars" were taken away! For what other class of scholars was the High School instituted? If it had not taken them away, it should indeed have been regarded, and justly, as a "failure."

The inference from this artful series of leading questions is irresistible, that it was Mr. Quincy's object to draw from the masters such a strong and united expression of opinions unfavorable to the High School for Girls as should seal its fate. He would thus accomplish *his* purpose; while upon *them* would fall the odium and responsibility of the act. I am well aware that, here and elsewhere, it is my misfortune to represent the character of Mr. Quincy, as a plain, frank, high-minded magistrate, in a questionable attitude, to use no stronger language. But for this I am not answerable. The *facts* are not of my making, they are on record. If the inferences are unjust or unwarranted, the opinion of an humble individual like myself will not give them currency.

But if Mr. Quincy wrote with these views, he mistook his men. With the exception of two or three, who responded as he probably wished and expected, the testimony for the teachers was, for the most part, in *favor* of the High School for Girls. However, Mr. Quincy proceeded to draw up a report, stating the "disadvantageous effects" of that institution on the other schools, and alluding to the *melancholy* and *unexpected* fact, that another class would demand admission in a few days!—whereat the reporter seems not a little puzzled,—as he cannot readily contrive how to bestow 130 girls in 130 seats already occupied! However, he is not yet "prepared to recommend that the High School should be abandoned, considering its apparent past success, and the general satisfaction of those who have enjoyed its benefits. He then goes on to recommend instead certain measures, which he *now* declares to have changed every one of the original features of the plan. He laments that, "instead of a High School, as originally projected for the admission of girls between eleven and fifteen years of age, none were to be admitted until they were fourteen; that instead of remaining three years, the course of instruction was limited to one year." Was the High School really instituted for the especial benefit of girls of eleven years of age, as the Mayor intimates when he speaks of the exclusion of "girls of eleven years of age, which was one of the *prominent* objects of its institution;" or has he seized upon an accidental circumstance, of little account or importance in itself, that one more item may be added to his list of "failures?" The original regulation, which required that a candidate should be of a specific age to entitle her to admission, was little better than absurd, and this vote made the matter worse. No limit of age should ever have been fixed, under which a girl might not be a candidate for admission. No restriction should have been prescribed excepting that of scholarship. To exclude a girl from admission to the schools in this city, where she would be daily subject to the care and control of her parents, simply because she is too young, is to inflict a penalty on industry and talents. I know not on what principle the rule in question can be defended, unless it be the true policy to deter children from making a rapid advancement in knowledge. Abolish this arbitrary rule,—let scholarship alone be required for admission into the higher schools,—and their influence would be more strongly felt in every part of the system.

It may be remarked that Mr. Quincy's apprehensions relative to the expense of maintaining a High School are quite groundless. In another community, it might be an effectual way to bring a valuable literary institution into disrepute by magnifying its expense; not so here. Besides, the grand mistake in all the Mayor's estimates, that "two High School-houses would be necessary the first year," lies in taking it for granted that every girl who makes application is entitled to admission into the High School. Nothing is more certain than that the School Committee might confine the operations of the High School for Girls to a single house for all coming time;—by keeping the standard of qualifications sufficiently high. "But," says Mr. Quincy, "in proportion as the qualifications for admission are raised, the school becomes *exclusive*, and though nominally open to all, is in fact open to the few." This is an idea upon which he evidently dwells with great complacency. That school must indeed have a strong hold upon the public confidence, which does not become odious and unpopular, when the Chairman of the School Committee, in his official capacity, openly proclaims the "*favoritism*" and "*selection*" and "*exclusion*" of the principles upon which it is based. Ought such epithets as these to be applied to the High School, because it was not designed that *all* the girls in Boston should acquire *all* their education in it? Is there either "selection," or "exclusion," or favoritism," in furnishing to every girl in the city exactly that kind and degree of instruction which she most needs? Mr. Quincy himself, in a communication made to the School Committee in 1826, recommending that a *thorough* knowledge of all the studies taught in the Grammar and Writing Schools should be re. quired for admission to the High School, says, "by an adherence to this system, it cannot be doubted that the High School will, in one or two years, become, *what it ought to be*, a school for the instruction in those parts of science to which the common schools are *from their constitutions inadequate, and for which they were not intended.*

Now in the face of all these facts and many others like them, some of which will be given, and all of which *shall* if necessary,—after all of these contrivances by which the "failure" of the High School was compassed, "*et quorum pars magna fui,*" Mr. Quincy may well say,—he next proceeds to talk about the "perfect fairness with which the experiment was conducted!" "for the most part under the same auspices which first adopted it!" The "changes" of which he speaks, have been proposed under the particular "auspices" of Mr. Quincy himself, and have been effected by his influence, authority and management,—yes, *management;* for he has in every instance when a committee was to be raised on the subject of the High School, either assumed the office of Chairman himself or appointed as Chairman some one supposed to be hostile to the institution. If there be any exception to this remark, it has not come to my knowledge, familiar as I am with the history of the school. At any rate the assertion is confidently and fearlessly made. If injustice is done, it can easily be shown, and it will give me pleasure to be convinced of my error.

As an example of the "perfect fairness" with which "the experiment was conducted," I will cite the course taken by the Mayor in regard to changing the hours of attendance at the High School. At the request of one hundred and seven of the parents of my scholars, I addressed a communication to the School Committee requesting that the school might have but one session, from 8 A. M. to 2 P. M., and giving a minute account of the reasons which led such an alteration of hours to be desirable. As soon as my letter had been read at the Board, Mr. Quincy hastily forestalled the remarks of other gentlemen, by expressing his decided disapprobation of "my very extraordinary proposition," as he was pleased to call it. One other member of the Committee was equally opposed to the change, and two others were doubtful as to its expediency; it was therefore determined to refer the subject to a special committee. Was it, as both usage and decorum required, referred to the sub-committee of the school? By no means; for they were in favor of the change, being well acquainted with the reasons for it. Mr. Quincy nominated a select committee for the purpose, *consisting of those three gentlemen who were not friendly to the measure proposed!* Two of them, however, became satisfied that the change was necessary, and reported accordingly; and the vote of the committee was nearly unanimous for accepting the report.

It has also been intimated that the High School was neglected, by these members of the committee, whose duty it was to watch over its interests and concerns. During the last year, it was not honored by a single visit from the sub-committee. The Chairman, Mr. Welsh, was in the room but twice, once when he introduced some members of the Legislature, and again when he came to witness the "Farce!" as he courteously termed the late exhibition. This speech came with peculiar propriety from the Chairman of the Committtee of the High School, and was the only one delivered on the occasion! If the "experiment" were an "entire failure," why was not that fact announced at the closing scene, when the attentive and crowded assembly,—numerous beyond all precedent in this city on a similar occasion, could have borne testimony to the wisdom and correctness of the decision? Again, when Mr. Quincy wrote to the masters of all the other public schools, demanding of them how many times they had been visited by their respective sub-committees, was it merely accidental that he omitted the master of the High School? I pause for a reply.

I will give one more instance of neglect. When the High School was instituted, the text-books for the first year only were determined. The higher classes having studied and reviewed all these, became impatient to commence the next studies in order. All verbal applications having proved of no avail, a letter was addressed to Mr. Quincy, urging in strong terms the necessity of immediate attention to this subject. After pressing my request, and waiting in vain for a long time, I took upon myself the responsibility of introducing such text-books as seemed best adapted to the course of studies marked out; otherwise the girls in the High School would not have had a single book to study during the whole of the last year! The extent of this responsibility may be learned from the fact, that any teacher who violates any of the regulations of the School Committee, shall immediately be dismissed; and these regulations provide that the books used in the public schools shall be "*such and such only* as shall have met the approbation of their respective sub-committees."

While the *visits* of the committee were "few and far between," the only written communication from the board with which I was honored for more than a year, was a letter from the Mayor, reprimanding me "in good set terms," because the young ladies, of their own free will and motion, had agreed among themselves to wear black silk aprons at the exhibition! And many of the communications which I made to the board from time to time, were so far honored as to be transferred to the hands of Mr. Welsh, and nothing more was done in the matter! The teachers of large public schools meet with so many daily trials and vexations, that they may feelingly say, "sufferance is the badge of all our tribe;" but when to these is added the marked hostility or contemptuous neglect of their employers, their duties become too irksome to be endured, unless they are either more or less than men.

While our worthy Mayor was making an array of instances in which the "original intention" of the Committee, in respect to the High School for girls "had failed," he might have added one case of *real* "failure" of some importance to the master at least. He might have said that the board "failed" to pay the salary which had been virtually promised, and which I had a right to expect. In establishing the High School, the intention of the Committee was distinctly expressed, that the master should be placed "in respect to salary upon a level with the masters of the Latin and English High Schools," who, it is well known, receive $2,000 a year. And when I became a candidate for the situation, it was with this understanding. It was suggested, however, that it would be safer to *begin* with a smaller salary, since, if the school were successful, it might easily be increased, and with these expectations, I was satisfied to accept the office with a salary of $1,500.

I am unwilling to speak of my services in the High School, yet may simply refer to their *amount* not to their *value*. The masters of the Latin and English High Schools have each under their immediate care from thirty to forty scholars; and each of them has several ushers to assist in the general superintendence of the school. I had under my sole care more than one hundred and thirty scholars, and in all circumstances was obliged to depend on my individual resources. Shall I be told that I had the assistance of scholars? So may every master have. But if the school had been badly conducted, would the scholars have been held responsible? I have no faith in the system which delegates the *authority* of the master to mere children, and *substitutes* the instruction and discipline of monitors for his personal services.

After the school had been fairly established, when the time for fixing the annual salaries approached, I requested the Committee to place mine on the basis originally proposed. I thought the request would be granted almost of course, but after a mature deliberation of several months, my letter was returned, with a very laconic endorsement upon it, that the request would not be granted! No reason was given for this very flattering and satisfactory decision. Indeed, I have never

yet heard any reason assigned why the master of the High School for girls should
be paid one quarter less or *any* less salary than is paid to the principals of the Latin
and English High Schools. His services *should* have been as valuable, his attainments as excellent and varied as theirs. The school undeniably *deserved* as good a
master as any in the city, and if the incumbent was not competent, it was a misfortune that might have easily been remedied.

But one course now remained for me—to send in my resignation, which I accordingly did in November, 1827. But I would beg leave to ask what would have
constituted a *successful* "experiment" according to Mr. Quincy's ideas upon the
subject? If the school had excited but little public interest—if few parents had
wished to send their daughters there—if the mode of government and instruction
had been unpopular—in a word, if its members, from any cause, had been so few
that a single room would have furnished the necessary accommodations for the
three annual classes, he would have regarded the experiment as completely successful! Should any one think this a distorted picture of Mr. Quincy's sentiments, I
beg him to read his report and judge for himself. But as the school happened to
be the reverse of all this, as the public voice was loud and emphatic in its favor,
as the strongest testimony possible was heard from almost every class in the community that such a school was wanted and demanded, the "experiment" is de-
nounced as "an entire failure," and the institution is to be annihilated, "as bodies
perish through *excess* of blood!"

In concluding this review, I would again repeat that I was not moved to under-
take it, either by personal interest or private feeling. It will readily be conceived
that this opposition to the High School for girls manifested by some of the most
influential members of the School Committee on all occasions, must have been a
deep source of mortification and regret to a man whose hopes were all centred in
its success, and who labored, regardless of fatigue and health and the pleasures of
society, to satisfy the wishes and expectations of its friends so far as his limited
abilities would permit. The *fact* of Mr. Quincy's hostility to the school is manifest, and his unfavorable account of the "experiment" will be respected accordingly. The integrity of his *motives* has not been questioned. Doubtless they have
been pure and conscientious; a difference in opinion is no proof of dishonesty.
But while it is granted that his opposition to the school may have been founded in
a sincere belief that the interests of the city do not require such an institution,
it cannot be denied, that in his zeal to put it down, he has suffered himself to pur-
sue a course of measures which we should not have expected from an intelligent
and high-minded magistrate.

BOSTON, 1828.   EBENEZER BAILEY.

•

EDUCATIONAL BIOGRAPHY; or Memoirs of Teachers, Educators, and Pro
moters and Benefactors of Education, Literature, and Science. By Henry
Barnard, LL.D. PART I. *Teachers and Educators.* Vol. I., United
States. NEW YORK: F. C. Brownell.

PRICE, $3.50, in half Turkish Morocco.

CONTENTS OF VOLUME I.

We are glad to see that Dr. Barnard has consented to let his publishers bring
together into one volume, the memoirs of eminent American Teachers and
Educators which have appeared in the first series of the *American Journal of
Education.* Richly bound, and illustrated with over twenty Portraits, from en-
gravings on steel or copper by our best artists, it is the most creditable tribute
which has yet been paid in English Literature to the scholastic profession. It
forms a splendid and appropriate gift-book to Teachers, and Promoters of Educational Improvement.—*Connecticut Common School Journal, for February,* 1859.

This elegant and useful contribution to educational literature will, we trust,
receive a cordial welcome from teachers. Nothing ever issued from the press
could be a more appropriate ornament for the teacher's library or center-
table.—*Massachusetts Teacher, for February,* 1859.

•